BOOK ONE:

Class Picture Day

LASHAWNDALE BONIER

To order additional copies of this book, contact:
Xlibris
844-714-8691
www.Xlibris.com
Orders@Xlibris.com

ISBN: Softcover   978-1-6698-0215-0
         EBook   978-1-6698-0214-3

Print information available on the last page

Rev. date: 01/20/2022

BOOK ONE:
CLASS
PICTURE
DAY

One morning Pinkie the Elephant woke up feeling very happy. He jumped out of his bed singing, "It's picture day. It's picture day." as he danced and laughed around his room. He rushed to the bathroom to get ready for school. He washed his hands and then his face. Pinkie smiled into the mirror when suddenly he realized he had lost a tooth.

"Oh... No! Where is my front tooth? It was there when I went to bed." Pinkie pointed to where his tooth use to be. "Oh where, oh where, why isn't my tooth there."

Mother Elephant heard her baby shout. She rushed to the bathroom to see what the cry was about.

"Pinkie, what's going on?"

"Mother, look." Pinkie once again pointed to the toothless spot.

"Oh Pinkie, your last baby tooth fell out. Everything is okay." Mother Elephant said with a smile. Pinkie frowned.

"But Mother, it's picture day at school. I can't take a picture with one tooth. I don't want to go to school."

"Why don't you want to go to school, Pinkie?" Mother Elephant asked.

"Because I will look different from everyone else. My friends aren't missing a tooth, and I am." Mother Elephant kneeled down in front of Pinkie and said.

"It is okay to look different and stand out, Pinkie. Everyone is different and special in their own way. Imagine how boring the world would be if everyone was the same. You are beautiful just as you are."

A knock at the door. Mrs. Elephant opened the door to Roland the Turtle. He is one of Pinkie's best friends from school.

"Hi, Mrs. Elephant." Roland greeted. Roland the Turtle is one of Pinkie's best friends from school. Mother Elephant greeted Roland in return.

"Hi Pinkie, We have to go, or we're going to be late for school. It's picture day! We can't be late, or we'll miss being in the class picture." Roland spoke excitedly.

Pinkie frowned in response. He did not want to school and did not want to be in the class picture. He feels embarrassed and doesn't want the other kids to laugh at him because of his missing tooth. But Pinkie knows that he can not miss school. So before leaving the house, he hugs his mother and grabs a large brown paper bag.

"Bye, Pinkie. Have a great day at school, and remember what I said. You are special and beautiful in your own way."

Pinkie nodded and followed Roland out of the door. He made two holes for his eyes and placed the paper bag overhead as they walked to school.

"Hey, what's wrong? Why are you wearing that paper bag over your head?" Roland asked.

"Oh... nothing, I just want to try something different this morning." Pinkie replied. Roland nodded and shrugged his shoulders in response.

As the two continued to school, they met with two more friends, Lola the Duck and Whootie the Owl.

"Whoooo's that under the large brown bag?" Whootie asked

"It's Pinkie the Elephant," Roland replied.

"Quack! Why do you have a bag on your head? Quack!" Lola questioned.

"Because I wanted to try something different for once." Pinkie replied with a huff.

As they continued to walk to their school. Lola, Roland, and Whootie thought it would be fun to try something different too.

"Hey, we should wear brown paper bags on our head too." the three shouted. They quickly stopped by the store and asked for large brown paper bags. They excitedly made two holes for their eyes and placed the brown paper bags over their heads before continuing their walk to school.

When the four friends made it to school, their classmates were all confused.

"Why are you wearing brown paper bags on your head?" Someone asked.

"Quack. It was Pinkie's idea. Quack." Lola answered.

"He wanted to try something different today, and we did too," Roland added.

"It's so much fun!" Whootie shouted. The rest of the class wanted to try something different and have fun too.

The classmates quickly found large paper bags and cut two holes for the eyes before placing them on their heads. Everyone laughed because it was different, but they all looked the same. Their teacher walked in and shrugged before leading the children to the gym for their picture time.

.As Pinkie stood amongst his peers... he looked left then right and frowned. He thought back to what his mother had said.

Now he could see it. There was nothing unique or different to set them apart because they all looked the same. Pinkie realized he wanted to be different. He really wants to stand out. He wants to stand out and be extra special in his own way. So as the cameraman counted down from three, Pinkie took off his brown paper bag and smiled real big.

Being different from everyone else is nothing to be ashamed about. It makes you unique and one of a kind. It makes you extraordinary in your own way.

Printed in the United States
by Baker & Taylor Publisher Services